TE HARÉ TU PROPIO LIBRERO
I'll Build You a Bookcase

TE HARÉ TU PROPIO LIBRERO
I'LL BUILD YOU A BOOKCASE

por/by Jean Ciborowski Fahey
ilustrado por/illustrated by Simone Shin
adaptado por/adapted by Yanitzia Canetti

Lee & Low Books Inc.
New York

Edited by Jessica V. Echeverria
Designed by Sheila Smallwood
Production by The Kids at Our House
The text is set in Latienne Medium
The illustrations are rendered in Acrylic and Digital
Manufactured in China by Jade Productions
Printed on paper from responsible sources
10 9 8 7 6 5 4 3
First Edition

Library of Congress Cataloging-in-Publication Data
Names: Fahey, Jean Ciborowski, 1949- author. • Shin, Simone, illustrator. • Canetti,
Yanitzia, 1967- translator. • Fahey, Jean Ciborowski, 1949- I'll build you a bookcase. •
Fahey, Jean Ciborowski, 1949- I'll build you a bookcase. Spanish. • Title: I'll build you
a bookcase = Te haré tu propio librero / by/por Jean • Ciborowski Fahey; illustrated
by/ilustrado por Simone Shin; adaptado al español por Yanitzia Canetti. • Other titles:
Te haré tu propio librero • Description: First edition. • New York: Lee & Low Books,
Inc., [2021] • Audience: Ages 4-6. • Audience: Grades K-1. • Parallel text in English
and Spanish. • Summary: Illustrations and rhyming text portray a loved one who
promises to build a home library to hold treasures that grow and change along with
their special child. • Identifiers: LCCN 2020030712 • ISBN 9781643794549 (hardback)
• ISBN 9781643792354 (board) • ISBN 9781643794600 (epub) • Subjects: CYAC: Stories
in rhyme. • Bookcases—Fiction. • Books and reading—Fiction. • Spanish language
materials—Bilingual. • Classification: LCC PZ74.3 .F33 2021 • DDC [E] —dc23 •
LC record available at https://lccn.loc.gov/2020030712

To my always loving and supportive husband, Tom

A mi siempre cariñoso y comprensivo esposo, Tom

—J. C. F.

To baby, Aydan

Para bebé, Aydan

—S. S.

I'll build you a bookcase before you are **born**
that's made out of boxes from shoes that were worn

Antes de que **nazcas**, te haré tu propio librero
con cajas de zapatos que se usaron primero

for books we will read in the soft morning light
and books we will read before saying good night.

para libros que leeremos con la suave luz temprana
y libros que leeremos antes del "hasta mañana".

I'll build you a bookcase for when you turn 1
with library books that are brimming with fun.

Te haré tu propio librero para cuando cumplas 1
con libros de biblioteca, divertidos cual ninguno.

We'll learn about bluebirds that live in a tree
and giant green turtles that nest near the sea.

De aves azules de un árbol, vamos a explorar,
y de tortugas gigantes que anidan junto al mar.

I'll build you a bookcase for when you turn **2**,
my phone tucked away so it's just me and you.

Te haré tu propio librero para cuando cumplas **2**,
mi teléfono bien lejos para oír solo tu voz.

We'll cuddle and snuggle—your heart next to mine.
You'll choose the same storybook for the tenth time.

Tu corazón junto al mío, bien juntitos, como ves.
El mismo libro de cuentos querrás por décima vez.

I'll build you a bookcase for when you turn **3**
for stories of faraway lands that we'll see—

Te haré tu propio librero para cuando cumplas 3
y cuentos de tierras lejanas vamos a leer después,

and castles on islands and treasures of gold.
The magic of reading will never grow old.

y de castillos en islas y de tesoros, y más.
La magia de la lectura no envejecerá jamás.

And let's build a bookcase for other kids too—
in parks and the Laundromat, even the zoo.

Y haremos un librero para otros niños también:
en parques, lavanderías y en zoológicos, ¡qué bien!

On sidewalks, at bus stops, all books will be free,
uptown and downtown, so many to see!

Los libros serán gratuitos en las paradas y aceras,
¡para que todos los vean en el centro o las afueras!

And then we can all read wherever we are,
perhaps on a rainbow or riding a star.

Y podremos leer en cualquier lugar después,
encima del arco iris o de una estrella tal vez.

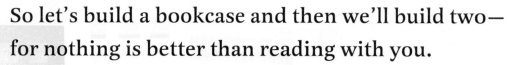

So let's build a bookcase and then we'll build two—
for nothing is better than reading with you.

Haremos un librero, luego dos vamos a hacer:
porque estando contigo, nada es mejor que leer.

HOW TO READ WITH YOUR CHILD – CÓMO LEER CON SU NIÑO

1. Have a small bookcase or dedicated space where your child can keep their books. You can borrow a number of diverse and culturally rich books from the library to start building your special bookshelf.

   Tenga un pequeño librero o dedique un espacio donde su niño pueda tener sus libros. Puede pedir prestados a la biblioteca libros diversos y culturalmente ricos para comenzar a construir tu librero especial.

2. Keep all the books at your child's height so they are easy to pick up and read.

   Mantenga todos los libros a la altura del niño para para que le sea fácil escogerlos y leerlos.

3. Let your child choose which book to read, even if it means rereading the same story countless times.

   Deje que su niño elija qué libro quiere leer, incluso si eso significa leer la misma historia muchas veces.

4. As you and your child read, track the words with your fingers. Touch the spot below each word as you say the word together.

   Mientras leen juntos en voz alta, sigan las palabras con los dedos. Señalen cada palabra mientras la dicen.

5. Read with expression! Make the stories come alive by changing your tone with the action or using a different voice for each character.

   ¡Lea con expresividad! Haga que las historias cobren vida cambiando tu tono de voz con cada acción o usando una voz diferente para cada personaje.

6. At the end of the story, share your favorite parts. What were your favorite characters, passages, illustrations, and new words? Why?

Al final de la historia, compartan sus partes favoritas. ¿Cuáles fueron los personajes, pasajes, ilustraciones y palabras nuevas que más les gustaron? ¿Por qué?

7. Make reading together a routine! Set aside a special time every day, even if it is just ten minutes. You might read together during breakfast, before naptime or bedtime, or while commuting on a train or bus.

¡Haga que leer juntos sea una rutina! Reserve un momento especial todos los días, incluso si son solo diez minutos. Podrían leer juntos durante el desayuno, antes de la siesta o la hora de acostarse, o mientras viajan en tren o autobús.

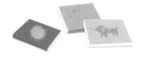

Lee & Low Books is dedicated to one mission:
publishing diverse books that all children can enjoy.

Lee & Low is proud to be the country's largest multicultural children's book publisher and one of the few minority-owned publishing companies in the United States. We publish culturally authentic books for young readers of all ages, with a wide selection of bilingual and Spanish titles. Our books connect all readers with our ever more diverse world. Lee & Low books are truly ABOUT EVERYONE and FOR EVERYONE.

For our complete catalog, free teacher's guides, interviews with our authors and illustrators, and other resources for our books, visit leeandlow.com.

Lee & Low Books
95 Madison Avenue • New York, NY 10016

JEAN CIBOROWSKI FAHEY is an author, parent educator, and speaker dedicated to promoting an early love of reading in children. She also consults for a variety of literacy initiatives and organizations and creates home literacy curriculum for parent-home visitors and early intervention specialists. She lives in Yarmouth Port, Massachusetts, with her husband, Tom, and dog, Indigo. Visit her online at readingfarm.net.

SIMONE SHIN is a children's book illustrator whose work is included in Lee & Low's poetry collection *I Remember: Poems and Pictures of Heritage.* Shin is the recipient of a Gold Medal from the Society of Illustrators, and her illustrations have appeared in the *New York Times, Real Simple, Wired,* and other publications. She lives in the San Francisco Bay area. You can see more of her work at simoneshin.com.